Thomas the Tank Engine & Friends

A BRITT ALLCROFT COMPANY PRODUCTION

Based on The Railway Series by The Rev W Awdry
© Gullane (Thomas) LLC 2002

Visit the Thomas & Friends web site at www.thomasthetankengine.com

All rights reserved. Published by Scholastic Inc.
555 Broadway, New York, NY 10012

ISBN 0-439-33852-2

12 11 10 9 8 7 6 5 4 3 2 1   2 3 4 5 6 7/0
Printed in the U.S.A.
First Scholastic printing, July 2002

This edition is available for distribution only through the direct-to-home market.

Mrs. Kyndley's Christmas

by
The REV. W. AWDRY

SCHOLASTIC INC.

New York   Toronto   London   Auckland   Sydney
Mexico City   New Delhi   Hong Kong   Buenos Aires

It was nearly Christmas. Annie and Clarabel were packed full of people and parcels.

Thomas was having very hard work.

"Come on! Come on!" he puffed.

"We're feeling *so* full!" grumbled the coaches.

Thomas looked at the hill ahead. "Can I do it? Can I do it?" he puffed anxiously.

Suddenly he saw a handkerchief waving from a cottage window. He felt better at once.

"Yes I can, yes I can," he puffed bravely. He pulled his hardest, and was soon through the tunnel and resting in the station.

"That was Mrs. Kyndley who waved to you, Thomas," his Driver told him. "She has to stay in bed all day."

"Poor lady," said Thomas. "I am sorry for her."

Engines have heavy loads at Christmastime, but Thomas and Toby didn't mind the hard work when they saw Mrs. Kyndley waving.

But then it began to rain. It rained for days and days.

Thomas didn't like it, nor did his Driver.

"Off we go, Thomas!" he would say. "Pull hard and get home quickly; Mrs. Kyndley won't wave today."

But whether she waved or not, they always whistled when they passed the little lonely cottage. Its white walls stood out against the dark background of the hills.

"Hello!" exclaimed Thomas' Fireman one day. "Look at that!"

The Driver came across the cab. "Something's wrong there," he said.

Hanging, flapping and bedraggled, from a window of the cottage was something that looked like a large red flag.

"Mrs. Kyndley needs help, I expect," said the Driver, and put on the brakes. Thomas gently stopped.

The Guard came squelching through the rain up to Thomas' cab, and the Driver pointed to the flag.

"See if a Doctor's on the train and ask him to go to the cottage; then walk back to the station and tell them we've stopped."

The Fireman went to see if the line was clear in front.

Two passengers left the train and climbed to the cottage. Then the Fireman returned.

"We'll back down to the station," said the Driver, "so that Thomas can get a good start."

"We won't get up the hill," the Fireman answered. "Come and see what's happened!"

They walked along the line around the bend.

"Jiminy Christmas!" exclaimed the Driver. "Go back to the train; I'm going to the cottage."

He found the Doctor with Mrs. Kyndley.

"Silly of me to faint," she said.

"You saw the red dressing-gown? You're all safe?" asked Mrs. Kyndley.

"Yes," smiled the Driver. "I've come to thank you. There was a landslide in the cutting, Doctor, and Mrs. Kyndley saw it from her window and stopped us. She's saved our lives!"

"God bless you, ma'am," said the Driver, and tiptoed from the room.

They cleared the line by Christmas Day, and the sun shone as a special train puffed up from the junction.

First came Toby, then Thomas with Annie and Clarabel, and last of all, but very pleased at being allowed to come, was Henrietta.

Sir Topham Hatt was there, and lots of other people who wanted to say "Thank you" to Mrs. Kyndley.

"*Peepeep, Peepeep!* Happy Christmas!" whistled the engines as they reached the place.

The people got out and climbed to the cottage. Thomas and Toby wished they could go, too.

Mrs. Kyndley's husband met them at the door.

Sir Topham Hatt, Thomas' Driver, Fireman, and the Guard went upstairs, while the others stood in the sunshine below the window.

The Driver gave her a new dressing-gown to replace the one spoiled by the rain. The Guard brought her some grapes, and the Fireman gave her some woolly slippers, and promised to bring some coal as a present from Thomas, next time they passed.

Mrs. Kyndley was very pleased with her presents.

"You are very good to me," she said.

"The passengers and I," said Sir Topham Hatt, "hope you will accept these tickets for the South Coast, Mrs. Kyndley, and get really well in the sunshine. We cannot thank you enough for preventing that accident. I hope we have not tired you. Good-bye and a merry Christmas."

Then going quietly downstairs, they joined the group outside the window, and sang some carols before returning to the train.

Mrs. Kyndley is now at Bournemouth, getting better every day, and Thomas and Toby are looking forward to the time when they can welcome her home.

Now flip the book over to start another Thomas & Friends adventure.

Daisy had an exhausting day. Toby and Percy often met her on their journeys, and though they never mentioned bulls, they gave her pitying looks. It made her so cross!

Her last journey ended at the top station. Some boys were on the platform. Suddenly one of them came running, holding a paper bag. "Look!" he shouted. "I've got a quarter of bull's-eyes. I think they're super, don't you?"

They shared the sweets and sucked happily.

"*Grrrrrh!*" said Daisy. "Keep your old bull's-eyes." She scuttled to her shed.

Now flip the book over to start another Thomas & Friends adventure.

Toby was surprised to find Daisy back once more at the station. The Passengers told him about the bull. He chuckled.

"Bulls *always* run if you toot and look them in the eye. Eh Daisy?"

Daisy said nothing.

"Ah well!" Toby went on. "We live and learn. I'd better chase him for you, I suppose."

He clanked away.

But Champion took no notice of Toby's bell or whistle. He didn't move till Toby "hooshed" him with steam. Then Toby gently "shooed" him along the track to where the Farmer and his men were waiting.

The Guard and the Policeman tried to "shoo" Champion. But he wouldn't stay "shooed." As soon as they turned away, he came back. He was a most inquisitive animal.

"Go on, Daisy," said her Driver. "He's harmless."

"Yes," said Daisy unhappily. "*You* know he's harmless, and *I* know he's harmless, but does *he* know? Besides, look at his horns. If I bumped into him he might hurt—er—them. The Farmer wouldn't like that."

Champion came close, and sniffed at Daisy. "*Ooof*," she said, backing hastily.

"*Uuuu Oooo!*" tooted Daisy. "Go on!"

Champion had his back to her. He was too busy to pay any attention.

"*Uuuuuuu Ooooooo!*" said Daisy again.

Champion went on eating.

"This is all wrong," thought Daisy. "How can I look him in the eye if he won't turn around? *Uuuuuuuuuu Ooooooooooo!*"

At last, Champion turned and noticed Daisy. "*Moooooooo!*" he said, and came towards her, still chewing. He wondered what she was.

"*Uuu Ooo!*" said Daisy feebly. "Why doesn't he run away?"

Champion wasn't really a fierce bull, but this morning he was cross. They had driven him away before he had finished breakfast, and tried to put him in a cattle-float. They had pulled him and pushed him, prodded and slapped him, but he wouldn't go.

He broke away, and trotted down the road. He saw a fence, jumped it, and slithered down a slope.

Champion was surprised. This was a new kind of field. It had a brown track at the bottom, but there was plenty of grass on each side, and he was still hungry.

"Even bulls," said Daisy confidently.

Daisy had never met a bull, but she purred away quite unconcerned. At the level-crossing, cars waited behind gates to let her pass. She tooted at a farm-crossing, and a horse and cart halted while she went by.

"Pooh," she said. "It's easy. I just toot, and they all stand aside. Poor little Toby! I *am* sorry he's frightened."

At the next station, a Policeman was waiting. "There's a bull on the line," he warned them. "Please drive it along towards the Farmer."

Daisy was excited. "Now," she thought, "I'll show Toby how to manage bulls."

Toby the Tram Engine has cowcatchers and sideplates. They help to prevent animals from getting hurt if they stray onto the line. Daisy thought they were silly. She said Toby was afraid of getting hurt himself.

"I'm not," said Toby indignantly.

"You are. *I've* not got stupid cowcatchers, but *I'm* not frightened. I'd just toot, and they'd all get out of the way."

"But they don't," said Toby simply.

"They would with me. Animals *always* run if you toot and look them in the eye."

"Even bulls?"

Bull's-Eyes

by
The REV. W. AWDRY

SCHOLASTIC INC.

New York   Toronto   London   Auckland   Sydney
Mexico City   New Delhi   Hong Kong   Buenos Aires